D0575921

The Royal Treasure Measure

To Pat Sorenson and Thann Hanchett —T.H.

To my lovely girls—Katarina and Milica—true measure of my life. . . —I.S.

Millbrook Press
A division of Lerner Publishing Group, Inc.
241 First Avenue North
Minneapolis, MN 55401 U.S.A.

Website address: www.lernerbooks.com

Main body text set in Klepto ITC Std 18/28.
Typeface provided by the International Typeface Corp.

Library of Congress Cataloging-in-Publication Data

Harris, Trudy, 1949-
The royal treasure measure / by Trudy Harris ; illustrated by Ivica Stevanovic.
p. cm. — (Math is fun!)
ISBN: 978-0-7613-6806-9 (lib. bdg. : alk. paper)
1. Weights and measures—Juvenile literature. 2. English language—Rhyme—Juvenile literature. I. Stevanovic, Ivica, ill. II. Title.
QC90.6.H37 2012
389'.62—dc23 2011045862

Manufactured in the United States of America
1 - DP - 7/15/12

By Trudy Harris   Illustrations by Ivica Stevanovic

M MILLBROOK PRESS • MINNEAPOLIS

Long before the lightbulb, the computer, plane, or car,

in a distant country lived a king named Balbazar.

The people of his kingdom had to measure in strange ways because there were no yardsticks or rulers in those days.

Tailors snipped and mended,
stitching day and night.
And even though they struggled,
the fit was never right.

Sire, your new robe shall be five candles long.

Roofers tried their hardest.
Builders did their best.
But all across the kingdom,
the people were distressed.

I'm sure I told him to make that door fourteen sausages high!

King Balbazar was worried.
The queen was quite distraught
until their conversation
gave Balbazar a thought.

Sausages? Spoons? Candles? What should the kingdom use?

If I knew the answer to that, these drapes would fit! Maybe we should just retire and let someone else decide.

If he could hold a contest,
perhaps he could retire
and leave behind the problems
that came with being sire.

Read ye! Read ye!

The one who solves
this riddle shall be king!

To find a treasure,
you'll need to measure
10 + 3 from the
walnut tree.

Go due west.
Do your best.
See what you can see.

P.S. The winner
will receive
Princess Star's
hand in marriage.

My hand?
NO WAY!
I'll pick my own
true love!
Well, we
do need someone
to judge the
contest. . . .

Wealthy men and peasants
arrived from every town.
They gathered at the nut tree
to try to earn the crown.

They measured using walnuts and broomsticks, swords, and sickles.

I'll bet the crown is buried. Maybe it's 10 over and 3 down.

There's nothing down here . . . down here . . . down here . . .

That knight
won’t win. Those
swords are all
different sizes.

They measured using rowboats
and cattle, goats, and pickles.

Grab those goats!
There's no treasure around here. Just ants.

A simple man named Arzo
resolved to try, but *how*?
He owned no sword or sickle
and not a single cow.

Shoes? Nope.
I don't have any.

Without a way to measure,
how could he compete?
He hung his head, and sadly
he stared down at his feet.

His feet!

Arzo started counting,
from one step up to ten.
To his right were bushes;
ahead were trees. And then . . .

at his left, a maiden.
Love at first sight bloomed.
But she was just a peasant.
His search for gold seemed doomed.

He took three steps toward her.
He gazed into her eyes.
Her smile became his treasure.
Then, quite to his surprise . . .

she reached inside her basket,
took out a golden crown,
and placed the crown on Arzo
as humbly he knelt down.

Later, they were married.
And in the village square,
the people learned to measure
when a sign was posted there.

Read ye! Read ye!

The official measurement of the kingdom shall now be the foot—exactly the size of King Arzo's foot.

No need to wonder.
No need to guess.
A foot is this long,
no more or no less:

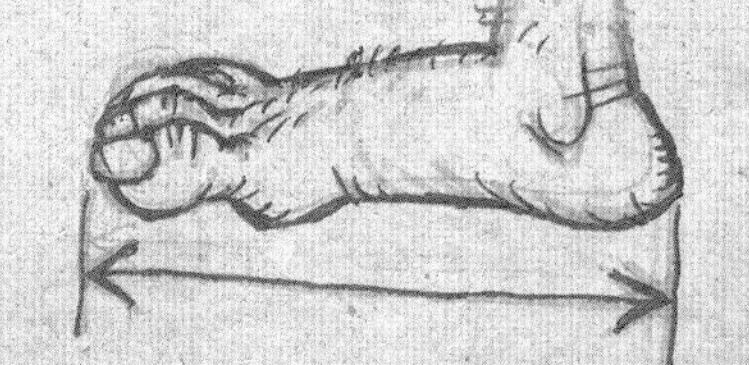

P.S. Queen Star has an idea for a special stick that will be the length of our new king's foot. In his honor, the stick will be called a ruler.

They lived happy ever after, Arzo and Queen Star.

And in a country cottage lived retired Balbazar.

Foot Note

No one knows for sure who first invented the "foot" measurement. However, many countries throughout the world have used measurements based on the length of a royal person's foot. Because feet vary in size, this measurement made trade between countries difficult. Sometimes, when a new king was crowned, measurements changed even within a country. In 1959, the international foot was established. It is equal to 0.3043 meters, with 3 feet in a yard and 12 inches in a foot. The international foot is definitely a better unit of measurement than sausages or candles!

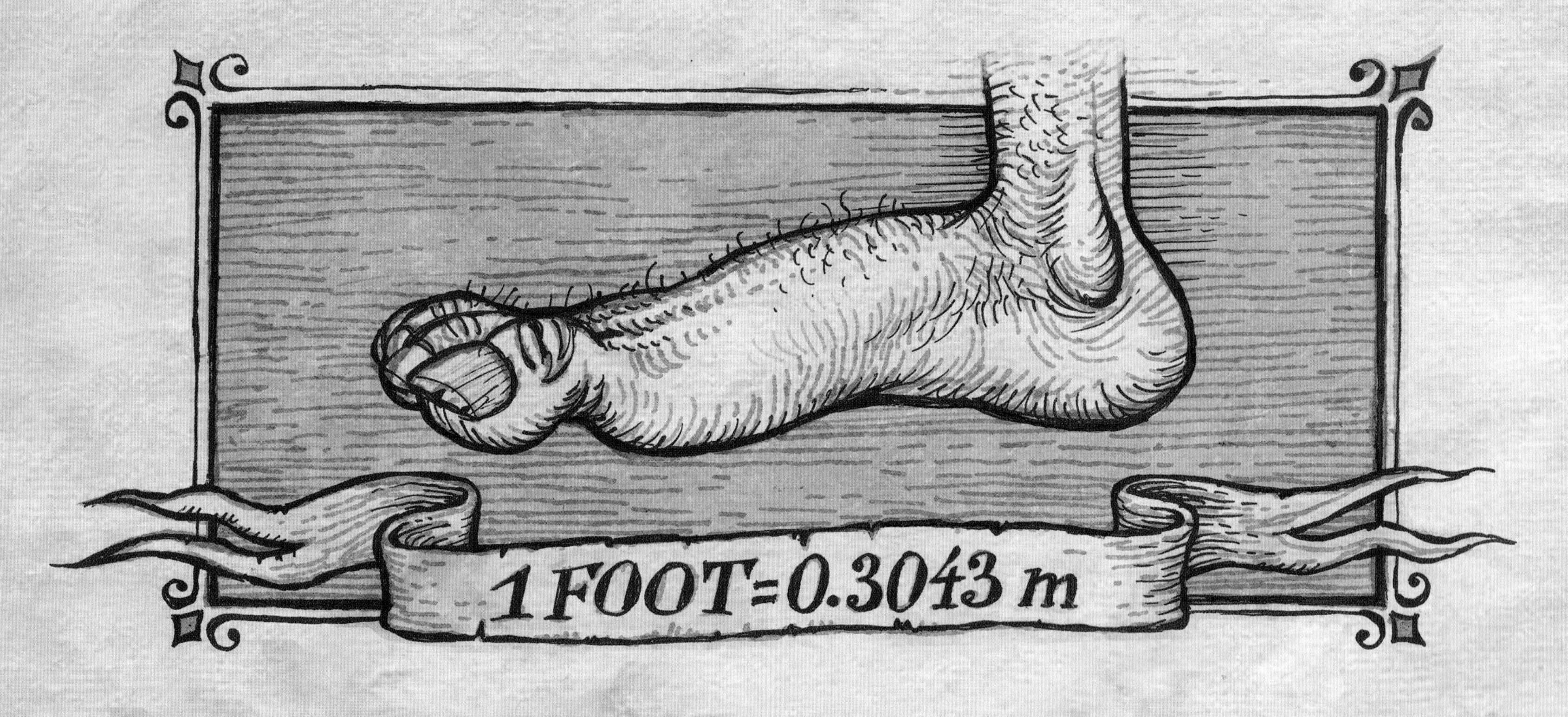